Clothes for a Summer Hotel

By TENNESSEE WILLIAMS

PLAYS

Baby Doll (a screenplay)
Camino Real
Cat on a Hot Tin Roof
Clothes for a Summer Hotel
Dragon Country
The Glass Menagerie
A Lovely Sunday for Creve Coeur
Small Craft Warnings
A Streetcar Named Desire
Sweet Bird of Youth
THE THEATRE OF TENNESSEE WILLIAMS, VOLUME I
  Battle of Angels, A Streetcar Named Desire, The Glass Menagerie
THE THEATRE OF TENNESSEE WILLIAMS, VOLUME II
  The Eccentricities of a Nightingale, Summer and Smoke, The Rose Tattoo, Camino Real
THE THEATRE OF TENNESSEE WILLIAMS, VOLUME III
  Cat on a Hot Tin Roof, Orpheus Descending, Suddenly Last Summer
THE THEATRE OF TENNESSEE WLLIAMS, VOLUME IV
  Sweet Bird of Youth, Period of Adjustment, The Night of the Iguana
THE THEATRE OF TENNESSEE WILLIAMS, VOLUME V
  The Milk Train Doesn't Stop Here Anymore, Kingdom of Earth (The Seven Descents of Myrtle), Small Craft Warnings, The Two-Character Play
THE THEATRE OF TENNESSEE WILLIAMS, VOLUME VI
  27 Wagons Full of Cotton and Other Short Plays
THE THEATRE OF TENNESSEE WILLIAMS, VOLUME VII
  In the Bar of a Tokyo Hotel and Other Plays
27 Wagons Full of Cotton and Other Plays
The Two-Character Play
Vieux Carré

POETRY

Androgyne, Mon Amour
In the Winter of Cities

PROSE

Eight Mortal Ladies Possessed
Hard Candy and Other Stories
The Knightly Quest and Other Stories
One Arm and Other Stories
The Roman Spring of Mrs. Stone
Where I Live: Selected Essays

Tennessee Williams

Clothes for a Summer Hotel

A Ghost Play

A New Directions Book

Manufactured in the United States of America

First published clothbound and as New Directions
Paperbook 556 in 1983

Published simultaneously in Canada by
George J. McLeod Ltd., Toronto

Library of Congress Cataloging in Publication Data

Williams, Tennessee, 1911–1983
Clothes for a summer hotel.
(A New Directions Book)
1. Fitzgerald, F. Scott (Francis Scott), 1896–1940,
in fiction, drama, poetry, etc.   2. Fitzgerald, Zelda,
1900–1948, in fiction, drama, poetry, etc.   I. Title.
PS3545.I5365C5   1983   812'.54   83-2360
ISBN 0-8112-0870-2
ISBN 0-8112-0871-0 (pbk.)

New Directions Books are published for James Laughlin
by New Directions Publishing Corporation,
80 Eighth Avenue, New York 10011

Clothes for a Summer Hotel

Clothes for a Summer Hotel was presented by Elliot Martin, in association with Donald Cecil and Columbia Pictures, at the Cort Theatre, in New York City, on March 26, 1980. It was directed by Jose Quintero; the scenic production was designed by Oliver Smith; costumes were by Theoni V. Aldredge; lighting was by Marilyn Rennagel; the original music was by Michael Valenti; and the dance consultant was Anna Sokolow. The cast, in order of appearance, was as follows:

GERMAN SISTER #1	MADELEINE LE ROUX
GERMAN SISTER #2	JOSEPHINE NICHOLS
GHOST	MARILYN ROCKAFELLOW
GHOST	TANNY MCDONALD
GHOST	GARRISON PHILLIPS
GHOST	SCOTT PALMER
GHOST	WEYMAN THOMPSON
GHOST	AUDREE RAE
F. SCOTT FITZGERALD	KENNETH HAIGH
GERALD MURPHY	MICHAEL CONNOLLY
BECKY	MARY DOYLE
ZELDA FITZGERALD	GERALDINE PAGE
JOURNALIST	ROBERT BAYS
PHOTOGRAPHER	SCOTT PALMER
NURSE #1	MADELEINE LE ROUX
INTERN	DAVID CANARY
SARA MURPHY	MARILYN ROCKAFELLOW
MADAME EGOROVA	AUDREE RAE
EDOUARD	DAVID CANARY
MRS. PATRICK CAMPBELL	JOSEPHINE NICHOLS
DOCTOR ZELLER	MICHAEL GRANGER
HEMINGWAY	ROBERT BLACK
HADLEY HEMINGWAY	TANNY MCDONALD
SINGER	WEYMAN THOMPSON
DANCER	MADELEINE LE ROUX
DOCTOR BAUM	MICHAEL GRANGER
NURSE #2	TANNY MCDONALD

This edition of *Clothes for a Summer Hotel* is a further revision, by the author, of the acting text published by Dramatists Play Service in 1981, which was itself a revision of the script of the Broadway production. The play now includes the following characters (in order of appearance):

F. SCOTT FITZGERALD
SISTER ONE
SISTER TWO
GERALD MURPHY
ZELDA FITZGERALD
INTERN
BECKY
SARA MURPHY
DR. ZELLER
BOO-BOO
HER NURSE
EDOUARD, played by the same actor as the INTERN
MRS. PATRICK CAMPBELL
ERNEST HEMINGWAY
HADLEY HEMINGWAY
A BLACK MALE SINGER
SEVERAL DANCERS
ASSORTED PARTY GUESTS

ııı

AUTHOR'S NOTE: This is a ghost play.

Of course in a sense all plays are ghost plays, since players are not actually whom they play.

Our reason for taking extraordinary license with time and place is that in an asylum and on its grounds liberties of this kind are quite prevalent: and also these liberties allow us to explore in more depth what we believe is truth of character.

And so we ask you to indulge us with the licenses we take for a purpose which we consider quite earnest.

THE SET: The stage is raked downward somewhat from the "mock-up" facade of Zelda's final asylum (Highland Hospital on a windy hilltop near Asheville, North Carolina) which is entered through a pair of Gothic-looking black iron gates, rather unrealistically tall. At curtain-rise there are three other set-pieces, a dark green bench downstage and, just behind it and slightly stage right of it, a bush of flickering red leaves that suggest flames; further downstage is a large rock which should seem a natural out-cropping on the asylum lawn, but which will later serve as a cliff above the sea in the scene between Zelda and Edouard.

Only the door of the asylum building is realistically designed for entrances and exits: the entire building must be in "sudden perspective" so that the third (top) floor of it—the one floor with barred windows, in which Zelda was confined with other patients taking insulin shock and in which she and the other shock patients were burned to "indistinguishable ash" in the autumn of 1947, years after Scott's death on the West Coast—is seen.

This must be regarded as a ghost play because of the chronological licenses which are taken, comparable to those that were taken in *Camino Real*, the purpose being to penetrate into character more deeply and to encompass dreamlike passages of time in a scene.

The windy hill was called Sunset, and the setting sun at the end of the play should be fierily reflected in the barred third floor windows.

The extent to which the characters should betray an awareness of their apparitional state will be determined more precisely in the course of a production.

At curtain-rise F. Scott Fitzgerald is standing before the mock-up building. He appears as he did when he died in his mid-forties, a man with blurred edges, a tentative manner, but with a surviving dignity and capacity for deep feeling.

SISTER ONE: If you are tired of waiting—

SCOTT [*cutting in*]: Yes, I am tired but I will continue to wait as long as she keeps me waiting.

[*There is a pause, the sound of wind.*]

SISTER TWO: There was a discussion among the staff lately about whether to paint the gates red to make them appear more cheerful.

SISTER ONE: To the patients and visitors. Do you think they should be painted red?

SCOTT: No.

SISTER ONE: Why?

SCOTT: I think it would make no perceptible difference.

SISTER ONE: The building is red.

SCOTT: *Is* it?

SISTER ONE: What?

SCOTT: Red.

SISTER ONE: Oh, yes, it is red, a dark red.

SCOTT: In some areas it appears to be black as if scorched by fire.

SISTER ONE: What did he say?

SISTER TWO: I didn't catch what he said—the wind blew his voice away.

SISTER ONE: And so that is your opinion?

SCOTT: What?

SISTER ONE: The gates should not be painted red to look cheerful?

SCOTT: Frankly speaking—

SISTER ONE: Yes?

SCOTT: If the objective is to create a cheerful impression, I would begin by removing the two of you from beside the gates.

SISTER ONE: Oh, no, we must guard them until they are locked for the evening.

SCOTT: Then why don't you wear red robes with dashes of white and blue. Sprinkle a few stars on them! Jesus!

[*Sister One crosses herself.*]

SISTER TWO: What did he say?

SISTER ONE: He spoke the name of our Lord.

[*Sister Two crosses herself. Gerald Murphy appears behind Scott.*]

MURPHY: It does no good antagonizing them, Scott.

SCOTT: Murph!

MURPHY: It will all be over in— [*He looks at his wristwatch.*] —one hour and forty-five minutes.

SCOTT: —It? [*Murphy nods. Scott staggers. Murphy catches his arm.*] Not drunk. Exhausted. You said "it"? —What is "it"?

VOICE BOOMING ON SPEAKERS: *La question est défendue.*

SCOTT: Is Sara with you, Murph?

MURPHY: Yes, she's gone back to the inn, you know, the Pine Grove Inn.

SCOTT: Yes. I know. —Dreary place for—

MURPHY: For a bit of rest. Pretty tired from the trip. Surprisingly long, considering . . .

SCOTT [*dazed, nodding in a bewildered way*]: Yes, I—

MURPHY: —She—she caught a glimpse of Zelda—practicing ballet.

SCOTT: Where?

3

MURPHY: Therapy room.

SCOTT: —Oh. Yes. —Excuse me, I'm—

MURPHY: You must have found it a long trip, too.

SCOTT: Long and—tiring. I'm only here for the afternoon and the night. [*Murphy nods.*] So. Sara saw Zelda, did she?

MURPHY: Saw her practicing—

SCOTT: Ballet . . .

MURPHY: Scott? Sara was so distressed, I'd better tell you this to prepare you when you see her. Scott, Sara—burst into tears. Scott? You ought to try to come out here more often, more for your own sake than hers. She has her fantasy world which we'll take part in later—

SISTER ONE: Thin ice.

SISTER TWO: Very thin ice.

[*The two men exchange wary glances. Scott clears his throat; Murphy kicks at some fallen autumn leaves.*]

MURPHY: I was going to say—oh, yes—working on the West Coast—right? [*Scott nods uncertainly.*] You see her rarely, now. So. The change you'll notice in her is going to be a shock. She's taking insulin; it's put a good deal of weight on her, and, well, regardless of what the doctors—

SCOTT: —I know—doctors . . .

MURPHY: They tell you what it's—

SCOTT: To their advantage, what's—expedient to tell you . . .

MURPHY: Of course that's understandable. You naturally realize that her reality is very different from ours even in these—circumstances.

SCOTT: She's still afflicted with that dancing craze, even now when any kind of a career, especially dancing, is—sadly—impractical.

MURPHY: Scott, we feel she was driven to it because—

SCOTT: I had to discourage her attempt to compete with my success as a writer: precocious, I face that now, have to bleed for it now. Have you seen Zelda's writing?

MURPHY: —Yes. That was her talent. I hear you made her promise not to publish *Save Me the Waltz* till your *Tender Is the Night* had come out.

SCOTT: Without apology, yes, I did. Didn't I have to pay for her treatment, for Scotty's Vassar and—I did. So much of Zelda's material was mine and she put it into her novel—a beautiful but cloudy, indistinct mirror of—

MURPHY: Yours! [*He turns away.*] I suppose all professional writers are self-protective first—and maybe last . . . [*He crosses offstage.*]

SCOTT: Where are you going, Murph? [*The reply is indistinct.*] They slip away from me now, dissolve about me . . . —Something strange here—unreal . . . disturbing!

ZELDA'S VOICE IN THERAPY: *Un, deux, pliez, un, deux, pliez,* etc.

[*Scott draws his coat collar about him, shivering.*]

5

SISTER ONE: The wind is cold on the hilltop; you could wait inside till she finishes her dancing.

SCOTT [*shouting*]: ZELDA! IT'S ME, SCOTT!

[*There is a slight pause.*]

ZELDA'S VOICE: —*Him? Impossible! —A dream* . . .

[*Another pause, then Zelda appears at the asylum doorway in a tutu and other ballet accoutrements, all a bit gray and bedraggled.*]

ZELDA: *For me, a visitor? Where?*

[*Murphy reappears, arrested by Zelda's outcry.*]

SCOTT: My God. Is that—? —Murph! Is that—?

MURPHY: Zelda.

SISTER ONE: Miss Zelda, get into your coat.

SISTER TWO: It's cold out.

ZELDA: I am not going out. Why would I go out?

SISTER TWO: Your visitor is waiting.

ZELDA: What visitor?

SISTER ONE: Your husband.

ZELDA: Impossible.

SISTER ONE: Look, he is by the bench.

ZELDA: No, no, no! An imposter! —No resemblance to Scott. [*She spins angrily about and rushes back into the asylum.*]

SCOTT: —That apparition was—! [*Scott covers his eyes.*]

MURPHY: Apparently she didn't recognize you either, Scott. You were a remarkably handsome young man, but—time has a habit of passing.

SCOTT: For me remorselessly—yes. . . . Murph, you mustn't leave me, I can't get through it alone!

MURPHY: Afraid you'd better.

SCOTT: I'd crack.

MURPHY: What's one more crack among all the others? I wouldn't think another would be very distinguishable from the rest.

SCOTT: —All right. God! —That was a beastly remark . . .

MURPHY: We are all obliged to make one now and then . . . [*He has retreated into the foliage, then calls back in a somewhat spectral voice.*] You and Zelda will be at our dance tonight at the villa? [*This line is almost drowned in the wind.*]

SCOTT: Dance? Where?

[*Zelda, wearing a coat, reappears at the asylum entrance with an intern.*]

ZELDA: How shall I play it?

7

INTERN: Delicately, delicately.

ZELDA: Delicacy is not the style of a hawk. [*She draws the coat tightly about her throat: her eyes are wide with shock.*]

SCOTT [*calling from downstage*]: Zelda, is that you?

ZELDA: Do I answer that pathetic mockery of my once attractive husband?

[*The intern nods, gripping her arm.*]

SCOTT: Come down where I can hear you! —I've waited hours!

ZELDA [*calling out*]: Hours, only hours. [*She turns to the intern.*] It's an impossible meeting, one that he would regret.

INTERN: Zelda, you must play it.

ZELDA: As if it existed?

INTERN: After a while, it will seem to exist.

ZELDA: I'll try to keep that in mind but the mind of a lunatic is not—retentive of present things. [*She advances slightly.*] You'll come to my assistance when I need you?

INTERN: Yes. Now go on out.

ZELDA: Why should this be demanded of me now after all the other demands? —I thought that obligations stopped with death!

INTERN: Zelda, you must go on.

ZELDA: I'm afraid.

8

INTERN: You've never known your courage.

ZELDA: I should be relieved of it now.

INTERN: Don't hold back! Don't let the dream dissolve. I'll follow a little behind you. You should receive him alone. *À bientôt.*

SCOTT [*calling*]: *Zelda?*

[*The intern exits into the asylum closing the doors behind him. Zelda begins a slow descent and moves downstage. Despite her increase of weight and the shapeless coat, her approach has the majesty of those purified by madness and by fire. Her eyes open very wide. Scott is barely able to hold his ground before their blaze. Zelda has to shout above the wind.*]

ZELDA: Is that really you, Scott? Are you my lawful husband, the celebrated F. Scott Fitzgerald, author of my life? Sorry to say you're hard to recognize now. Why didn't you warn me of this—startling reunion, Scott?

SCOTT: I had to come at once when the doctors advised me of your remarkable improvement.

ZELDA: —Not exactly an accurate report. —Aren't you somewhat unseasonably dressed for a chilly autumn afternoon?

SCOTT: When I got the doctors' report, well, I forgot the difference in weather between the West Coast and here, just hopped right onto the first plane—bought a spare shirt at a shop at the airport.

ZELDA: I see, I see, that's why you're dressed as if about to check in at a summer hotel.

SCOTT: It's all right, Zelda.

ZELDA: Is it all right, Scott?

SCOTT: Since I have to fly back tomorrow. —Don't be so standoffish, let me kiss you.

[*He goes to Zelda and tentatively embraces and kisses her in a detached manner.*]

ZELDA: —Well.

SCOTT: I would describe that as a somewhat perfunctory response.

ZELDA: And I'd describe it as a meaninglessly conventional—gesture to have embraced at all—after all . . . [*He draws back wounded: she smiles, a touch of ferocity in her look.*] —Sorry, Goofo. It's been so long since we've exchanged more than letters. . . . And you fly back tomorrow? We have only this late afternoon in which to renew our—acquaintance.

SCOTT [*uncomfortably*]: Work on the Coast, film-work, is very exacting, Zelda. Inhumanly exacting. People pretend to feel but don't feel at all.

ZELDA: Don't they call it the world of make-believe? Isn't it a sort of a madhouse, too? You occupy one there, and I occupy one here.

SCOTT: I'm working on such a tight schedule. Never mind. Here's the big news I bring you. I'm completing a novel, a new one at last, and it will be one that will rank with my very best, controlled as *Gatsby* but emotionally charged as *Tender Is the—*

[*Pause.*]

ZELDA: —Good . . . will I be in it?

SCOTT: Not—recognizably . . .

ZELDA: Good. —So what is the program for us now? Shall we make a run for it and fall into a ditch to satisfy our carnal longings, Scott?

SCOTT: That was never the really important thing between us, beautiful, yes, but less important than—

ZELDA [*striking out*]: *What was important to you was to absorb and devour!*

SCOTT: I didn't expect to find you in this—agitated mood. Zelda, I brought you a little gift. A new wedding band to replace the one you lost.

ZELDA: I didn't lose it, Scott, I threw it away.

SCOTT: Why would you, how could you have—?

ZELDA: Scott, we're no longer really married and I despise pretenses.

SCOTT: I don't look at it that way.

ZELDA: Because you still pay for my confinement? Exorbitant, for torture.

SCOTT: You always want to return here; you're not forced to, Zelda.

ZELDA: I only come back here when I know I'm too much for Mother and the conventions of Montgomery, Alabama. I am pointed out on the street as a lunatic now.

SCOTT: Whatever the reason, Zelda, you do return by choice,

11

so don't call it confinement. And even if you don't want a new marriage ring, call it a ring of, of—a covenant with the past that's always still present, dearest.

ZELDA: I don't want it; I will not take it!

SCOTT [*with a baffled sigh*]: Of course we do have nonmaterial bonds, memories such as— "Do you remember before keys turned in locks—when life was a close-up, not an occasional letter—how I hated swimming naked off the rocks—but you liked nothing better?"

ZELDA: No, no, Scott, don't try to break my heart with early romantic effusions. No, Goofo, it's much too late!

SCOTT: I wasn't warned to expect this cold, violent attitude in you!

ZELDA: Never in all those years of coexistence in time did you make the discovery that I have the eyes of a hawk which is a bird of nature as predatory as a husband who appropriates your life as material for his writing. Poor Scott. Before you offered marriage to the Montgomery belle, you should have studied a bit of ornithology at Princeton.

SCOTT: I don't believe a course in ornithology was on the curriculum at Princeton in my day!

ZELDA [*distracted, looking vaguely about*]: What a pity! You could have been saved completely for your art—and I for mine . . .

SCOTT: Didn't hear that, the wind blows your voice away unless you shout. Is it always so windy here?

[*The wind blows.*]

ZELDA: Sunset Hill on which this cage is erected is the highest to catch the most wind to whip the flame-like skirts as red as the sisters' skirts are black. Isn't that why you selected this place for my confinement?

[*Scott moves toward her, extending his arms and gesturing toward the bench.*]

Are you studying ballet, too?

SCOTT [*attempting to laugh*]: Me, studying ballet?

ZELDA: You made a gesture out of classic ballet, extending your arms toward me, then extending the right arm toward that bench which I will not go near—again.

SCOTT: Now, now, Zelda, stop play acting, come here!

ZELDA: I won't approach that bench because of the bush next to it. Besides I'm only taking a little recess from O.T.

BECKY [*offstage voice*]: The head of the Harlow, the platinum of it, the bleach! —My personal salon was only a block from Goldwyn's . . .

[*Zelda starts drifting back to the doorway of the asylum. Scott grabs her.*]

SCOTT: *Zelda, don't withdraw!*—What are you— Tell me, Zelda, what are you working on mostly in Occupational Therapy now, dear?

ZELDA: The career that I undertook because you forbade me to write!

SCOTT: Writing calls for discipline! Continual!

ZELDA: And drink, continual, too? No, I respect your priority in the career of writing although it preceded and eclipsed my own. I made that sacrifice to you and so elected ballet. Isadora Duncan said, "I want to teach the whole world to dance!" —I'm more selfish, just want to teach myself.

SCOTT: The strenuous exercises will keep your figure trimmer.

ZELDA: Than writing and drinking?

SCOTT: Oh, I've quit that.

ZELDA: Quit writing?

SCOTT: Quit drinking.

ZELDA: QUIT? DRINKING?

SCOTT: Completely.

ZELDA: Cross your heart and hope to die?

SCOTT: I cross my heart but I don't hope to die until my new book is finished. [*Scott has maneuvered Zelda toward the bench. He sits and gets her to sit.*] Zelda, I've had—several little heart disturbances lately . . .

ZELDA: You mean the romance? Or romances?

SCOTT: I mean—cardiac—incidents. At a movie premiere last week, as the film ended, it all started—fading out . . .

ZELDA: Films always end with the fade-out.

SCOTT: I staggered so. I thought the audience would think I was drunk.

14

ZELDA [*sarcastically*]: Were they as foolish as that?

SCOTT: Luckily I had a friend with me who helped me out.

ZELDA: Oh, yes, I know about her.

SCOTT: You—she—you'd like her.

ZELDA: Certainly, if you do. Well—Scott? Let me say this quickly before I become disturbed and am hauled back in for restraint. You were not to blame. You needed a better influence, someone much more stable as a companion on the—roller-coaster ride which collapsed at the peak. You needed—*her?* Out there, utterly vulgar but—functioning well on that level.

SCOTT: Who are you, what are you—referring to, Zelda?

ZELDA: Who or what, which is it? Some are whats, some are whos. Which is she? —Never mind. You are in luck which-ever. . . . But can we turn this bench at an angle that doesn't force me to look at the flaming bush here?

SCOTT: It's such a lovely bush.

ZELDA: If you're attracted by fire. Are you attracted by fire?

SCOTT: The leaves are—radiant, yes, they're radiant as little torches. I feel as if they'd warm my hands if I—

ZELDA: I feel as if they'd burn me to unrecognizable ash. You see, the demented often have the gift of Cassandra, the gift of—

SCOTT: The gift of—?

ZELDA: Premonition! I WILL DIE IN FLAMES!

15

SCOTT: Please, Zelda, don't shout, don't draw attention. The doctors will think my visits disturb you—I won't be allowed to come back.

ZELDA: Visits? Did you say visits? That is plural. I wouldn't say that your presence here today qualifies as a very plural event.

[*She starts toward the gates. Scott rises to follow.*]

SCOTT: You're going inside?

ZELDA: I have my own little Victrola. Mama sent it to me for Christmas. I'm preparing for Diaghilev; he's offered me an audition. I'm going to do a Bach fugue with almost impossible *tempi* I was told. *Hah!*

SCOTT: Zelda, I didn't come all the way out here to listen to a Bach fugue, and watching you dance is a pleasure I've—exhausted . . .

ZELDA: Sorry. But I'm working against time! [*She continues imperiously.*] Sister, Sister, I want my little Victrola; my husband wants to see the dance I'm preparing for my audition for Diaghilev this—

SISTER ONE: You'll have to bring it out.

SISTER TWO: Or bring your visitor in.

SISTER ONE: We have to stay at the gates.

ZELDA: Oh, God damn you, bitches, all right, I'll fetch it out myself! Scott, wait! The idiot teacher, fuck her, said the *tempi* were impossible for me! I'll show her!

SCOTT: You'll come back out?

[*Zelda's voice is lost in the wind as she rushes to the entrance of the asylum. Scott speaks to the sisters.*]

She never spoke that way, never, never vulgarly before.

SISTER ONE: In an asylum they talk, they scream like that.

SISTER TWO: They pick it up from each other.

SCOTT: She didn't ever.

SISTER ONE: The excitement of your visit she did not expect. If I were you—

BECKY [*offstage voice, shouting*]: My personal salon! Transferred heads of stars!

SISTER TWO: Look who's coming back out! Shall I stop her?

[*Sister One shrugs. Becky appears in the doorway and moves to the middle of the platform.*]

Now what is it, Becky?

BECKY: I'm not talking to you so shut up. [*She sees Scott and calls to him.*] Mister? You, Mister?

[*Scott retreats downstage near the rock below the bench. Becky moves around the bench and then toward Scott.*]

You're from Hollywood, aren't you? Yes? Somebody said so! I am, too! My salon was a block from Goldwyn. Dressed hair for gentlemen, too. The Navarro! Was called to Falcon's Lair for the great Valentino, the Sheik!

SCOTT: Not now, not necessary, no time, just—visiting my—

17

[*Zelda reappears from the asylum, lugging a portable wind-up Victrola.*]

Zelda, please! Can't somebody restrain this—

ZELDA: Fight them off, you've got to fight them off! Hit her, give her a—

SCOTT: A demented woman, I—

ZELDA: Can't? Ungentlemanly? Well, look. I can, I can! [*She delivers a blow to Becky who kicks back at her.*] In, in, get this lunatic in!

[*Becky is captured by the sisters and herded into the mock-up asylum.*]

SCOTT: Distressing—distressing that you are exposed to—have to associate with—

ZELDA: Please wind up my Victrola. Dr. Bleumer, is that the name, have I got the name right? —He thought they would draw me out. "Mrs. Fitzgerald, converse with the other ladies." —There was a fake countess, there was a pretender to the throne of— [*She laughs harshly.*] —something! —"Dr. Bleumer," I said, "I have no social ambitions whatsoever." —Oh, God, Scott, can't you even wind a Victrola?

[*Gerald and Sara Murphy appear from the wings.*]

I'm working against time, only a week to prepare for my audition for—DIAGHILEV! Ballet Russe de—

MURPHY: Don't let her see you crying!

ZELDA [*rushing to the Murphys*]: Sara! Gerald!

18

SARA [*embracing her*]: Darling! We just dropped by to—

MURPHY: We happened to be in—

ZELDA [*hallucinating*]: Paris? On your way to St. Rapheal? Where is Mme. Egorova? Secretly tipples a bit but such a wonderful, wonderful instructor of classic ballet. [*She calls out.*] *MADAME? MADAME? MES AMIS LES MURPHYS SONT ICI POUR—* Gerald, Scott's in a daze! Would you please wind up my Victrola? Mme. Egorova feels I've embarked upon a dance career rather late in life, but she says that with such application and such longing, such dedication, I can make up for delay. You know that old poem? "She that comes late to the dance/more wildly must dance than the rest/though the strings of the violins/are a thousand knives at her breast."

SARA [*sotto voce*]: Start the Victrola for her, we'll act it out.

SCOTT: No, no, don't encourage—hallucinations, I wasn't advised—correctly . . .

[*But a Bach partita is now playing and Zelda is dancing. Gerald Murphy holds Sara's hand tightly as Sara holds a handkerchief to her nostrils. Zelda stumbles to the ground.*]

SARA: Oh, Zelda!

ZELDA: I'm all right. It was the *pizzicato*, most difficult part of—but I'm—determined: must master it for Diaghilev next week.

MURPHY: The poor child, she received no offer except from the *Moulin Rouge* . . .

SARA: Shhh! Shout *"Brava!"*

19

MURPHY: *Brava! Bravissima!*

SCOTT: You think it kind to encourage hallucination? Excuse me, I don't agree! The doctors who called me out here, cross-country despite heart condition, have ignored my requests for consultation about her. [*He rushes to the door of the mock-up asylum.*] Doctor! Doctor! Bleumer!

SARA [*to Murphy*]: I'm afraid!

MURPHY: It won't go?

SARA: Scott will break it down. Couldn't you prepare him?

MURPHY: Tell him that—?

SARA: Something, anything.

MURPHY: Couldn't! Which of them suffered more?

SARA: Wasn't there a woman with him on the Coast?

MURPHY: Yes, but—we know the compromises Scott had to make and finally—almost the indignity of Chekhov's body returned to Russia in a freight car labeled—"Oysters". . . . If anybody's discovered dignity in death—

[*The intern, who will also appear as Edouard, appears at the asylum door in response to Scott's shouts.*]

Oh, it may be reported as having "occurred quietly" in sleep, and so forth, but—the only reliable witness is the deceased, and reports by the deceased aren't—publicly reported.

SCOTT [*to the intern, advancing to the gates*]: Who are you? Surely you're not Dr. Bleumer, why, you look like—

20

MURPHY: If he should recognize him as—

SARA: Edouard?

MURPHY: It will all explode.

SCOTT: Well, whoever! Did you see her out there?

INTERN: Zelda?

[*Zelda, in a frozen position, stares at the intern, fist pressed to her mouth.*]

SCOTT: Please refer to my wife as Mrs. Fitzgerald, not— Zelda . . .

INTERN: We call patients by the first name to create an intimacy with them to make them feel they're at home.

SCOTT: Her home's not here. And not in a—long-ago ballet studio in Paris.

INTERN: Isn't it where she prefers it? If offering her some comfort is the object?

SCOTT: You're not Dr. Bleumer? Nor Zeller?

INTERN: No, no, just an intern, but all of us here are acquainted with Zelda's case, the tragedy she's borne with such—gallantry, *monsieur.*

SCOTT: I see. I hope that I see. —BUT I was falsely informed that she had nearly recovered, flew out from the Coast to make sure—and discover what? More demented than ever, and now violent, too. Look, you. I want to tell you something! —I've sold, am selling my talent, bartering my life and my daughter's future

21

in the obviously vain hope that—here at Highland you could—
[*He covers his face for a moment.*] —return her to—

INTERN: What?

SCOTT: *REASON, REASON, GOD DAMN IT!* What the
hell else did you offer?

[*Zelda has started advancing slowly to Scott and the intern.*]

INTERN: A refuge.

ZELDA: I AM NOT A SALAMANDER! —Just tell him that.

[*Murphy has led Sara off.*]

INTERN: Salamander, she said?

SCOTT: The salamander does not exist, never did; it is a mythological creature that can live in fire and suffer no hurt or—
[*Scott utters a gasp, almost a sob.*] —injury from—the element
of fire.

ZELDA: I am not a salamander. Do you hear? You've mistaken
my spirit for my body! Because my spirit exists in fire does not
mean that my body will not be consumed if caught in fire behind
barred gates and windows on this windy hill.

[*Zelda, trembling, faces the two men: she looks from one to
the other with wild, imploring eyes.*]

INTERN: Salamander, sal-a-mander. Hmm. We've heard her
refer to a salamander before but no one seems to know what she
is talking about.

SCOTT: By no one you mean yourself and the patients? You

22

surely don't mean the doctors! Why, doctors are men of education, I thought! Such a degree of illiteracy doesn't exist among—men of science.

INTERN: By none of us of course I spoke for the staff at Highland.

SCOTT: You've heard my wife repeatedly refer to a salamander and yet you stand there and tell me that not a goddam one of you bothered to look it up!

[*The doctor appears behind the intern.*]

DR. ZELLER: Is there some trouble? Can I be of assistance?

SCOTT: You are—

DR. ZELLER: Dr. Zeller. You are Zelda's husband?

SCOTT [*furiously*]: I am sometimes known, in fact I am usually known—perhaps because I haven't been in the right places—as F. SCOTT FITZGERALD!

DR. ZELLER: Ahh? You are the husband?

SCOTT: You receive my monthly checks and still you don't know who I am?

[*The intern is supporting Zelda.*]

Tell that impertinent young—

DR. ZELLER: Since I am in consultation, staff meeting, tell quickly the trouble, *bitte*!

VOICE [*offstage, calling*]: Dr. Zeller?

23

DR. ZELLER: *Ja*—yes, *ein Moment!* You see . . . and so?

INTERN: He has disturbed his wife. She started to collapse.

DR. ZELLER: Give her—reassurance. She deserves comfort.

INTERN [*to Zelda*]: *Mieux, maintenant? Ma chère?*

ZELDA: I don't want to hurt him, I never wanted to hurt him. But tell him I am—not—a salamander.

DR. ZELLER: *Ach, der Salamander!* You see, being German, the word is not the same to me, I do not know what it is.

SCOTT: German, French—someone here must be English-speaking. Is no one English-speaking? To look up the word "salamander"?

DR. ZELLER: I will ask Dr. Baum who is more English-speaking to, to—what?

SCOTT: LOOK UP THE WORD! OTHERWISE HOW CAN YOU UNDERSTAND WHAT SHE MEANS BY IT?

DR. ZELLER [*to the intern*]: *Betrunken?*

SCOTT: Since it is obvious that she's obsessed with fire for some reason and keeps crying out "I am not a salamander," one of you might bother to look it up! —It's—mythological—meaning . . .

INTERN: In what?

SCOTT: A DICTIONARY, goddam it . . .

DR. ZELLER: *Ja, BETRUNKEN.* —Offer him a cold shower. I must go in. [*He enters the asylum.*]

INTERN: Of course. *Soyez un peu plus calme pour la visite, Monsieur*—Fitzgerald. —Would it help to have a cold shower as Dr. Zeller—suggests?

SCOTT: Thinks me drunk!

ZELDA: A frequent—misapprehension. Seems like—old times, Scott.

SCOTT: *UNBEARABLE!*

ZELDA: Yes, that's life for us, Goofo. —Did I say life? I tried to understand, I did, I did so hard.

INTERN: *Pauvre homme.* I was always concerned. Wondered what effect the indiscretion—

SCOTT: To be ridiculed, called drunk when Sheilah won't permit me to touch liquor.

ZELDA: Then the West Coast companion is better for you, Goofo.

SCOTT: Salvaging what's left of— [*He fumbles in his pocket.*] —Left my nitro? —No, wouldn't dare. —Little bottle of tablets for—man with heart condition, induced by false report to fly across country and witness this—

INTERN: Here it is. In this pocket. Now come in for—

SCOTT: NOT DRUNK! —DON'T NEED SHOWER! FREEZING COLD ON THIS WIND TOP!

INTERN: Just rest—Mr. Fitzgerald.

SCOTT: Yes, I—work mostly in bed . . .

[*Zelda utters a barely audible laugh. The intern/Edouard has seated Zelda on the bench. Then he places an arm about Scott and leads him toward the entrance of the mock-up asylum.*]

Don't touch me—can move—unassisted. But tell them all, the whole money-grubbing, lying staff of the—I will not—where's Zelda?

[*The voices are quieter: there is faint, elegaic music.*]

INTERN: Recovering from the disturbance of your unexpected visit.

SCOTT: Oh, but I won't leave without discovering who's responsible for my wife's deteriorating condition, *MUST!* LEARN!

INTERN: And if you learn it is *you*?

SCOTT: You're taken in, all of you, by her crazed accusations?

[*They enter the asylum. Zelda rises from the bench and crosses to the proscenium. Her eyes make it apparent she is about to attempt to make a meaningful statement. Author's note: In this scene Zelda must somehow suggest the desperate longing of the "insane" to communicate something of their private world to those from whom they're secluded. The words are mostly blown away by the wind: but the eyes—imploring though proud—the gestures—trembling though rigid with the urgency of their huge need—must win the audience to her inescapably from this point through the play: the present words given her are tentative: they may or may not suffice in themselves: the presentation—performance—must.*]

ZELDA: There's something I— [*The wind sound comes up and drowns her voice, then subsides.*] —But the winds, the winds, this continual—lamentation of winds as if— [*The wind sound rises again and subsides.*] —they were trying to give one single tongue to all our agonies here. . . . Oh, but I write home cheerful letters to reassure Mother, lonely, family scattered to—winds. . . . Speak of pleasant strolls through the hills, not mentioning the escort of female dragons keeping us in line, bearing straps to restrain us if we—attempt to break ranks—ha, ha. . . . No need to distress her with actualities now. At our last parting in Montgomery, I said to her as I left, "Don't worry, Mother. I'm not afraid to die." —Not knowing how it would happen.

[*The upper stories light with flame and she cries out, crouching, hand to her eyes. There is the ghostly echo of women burning at a locked gate. The intern/Edouard, the doctor, the two sisters, all rush toward her. Zelda waves them away.*]

Sorry, nothing happened, it was a trick of light . . .

DR. ZELLER: May we continue without disturbance of this kind.

ZELDA: For what purpose? I don't understand the purpose.

DR. ZELLER [*to intern*]: Explain!

ZELDA: Yes, do! —Explain the inexplicable to me, please.

[*All except the intern/Edouard withdraw.*]

INTERN: Shadows of lives, tricks of light, sometimes illuminate things.

ZELDA: Not to us. To audiences of a performance of things past. Wasn't there once a little *auberge*, the *Reve Bleu*—where I cried out so wildly in your embrace that you were shocked and abandoned me to this long retreat into—

[*An idiotically cheerful white-starched nurse wheels a patient, Boo-Boo, up to Zelda.*]

this . . .

NURSE: Boo-Boo saw her roommate and wanted to say hello.

[*The spectral Boo-Boo is past all "wanting."*]

ZELDA: Hello, Boo-Boo—bye-bye—Boo-Boo.

[*Bells ring inside the asylum as the nurse wheels Boo-Boo that way.*]

Five o'clock—feeding time at the zoo . . .

[*As if sadly sensing a failure to receive them properly into her haunted world, Zelda offers the audience a polite social smile and a slight bow as—*]

THE LIGHT DIMS OUT

SCENE TWO

The table is pre-set with a bulletin board with a chart and several clippings attached with thumb tacks, sharpened pencils, and a book or two.

The music for this change ends and Scott, wearing a white knit sweater, enters from the rear of the stage. He was the most methodical of writers, charting out the course of a work in progress with the most astute care.

Zelda is dimly visible at the edge of the lighted area (behind Scott) looking as she did in about 1926. She advances into the scene more clearly when she speaks.

SCOTT [*setting a gin bottle on the table*]: There! Christ—when a writer starts drinking at work—who was it said he's only got ten years to go? Oh, yes—Galbraith, who never really got started.

[*He pours himself half a tumbler of gin and regards it moodily. Then he touches his slender waist.*]

—Hasn't put fat on me yet—but there's time. Hemingway's still in good shape and drinks more than me. —Or does he? —There's time . . . [*He settles down to work at the table.*] No more decor, surface of the work, too damn easy for me. Chapter Five is where it must begin to bite hard and deep.

[*Zelda approaches the table.*]

ZELDA: Dear Scott, dear Goofo—"bite hard and deep"—are you writing about a shark, a tiger—a hawk—or a human composite of all three?

SCOTT: —How long have you been standing back there, Zelda?

ZELDA: Just crept in against orders, to admire you at work.

29

[*He shuts his eyes tight for a moment.*]

SCOTT: I don't work to be admired at it.

ZELDA: I know, for the work to be admired. But, Goofo, you look so pretty working, at least till— [*She points at the bottle.*]

SCOTT [*still facing front*]: Pretty did you say?

ZELDA: Admirable, and pretty. At first, you know, I had reservations about marriage to a young man prettier than me.

SCOTT: Than you?

ZELDA: I'm not pretty, only mistaken for it. [*Her eyes are dark, tender, disturbed.*] But, Goofo, you really *are*.

SCOTT [*with an edge*]: Don't keep on with that, Zelda, that's insulting.

ZELDA [*approaching him, touching his throat*]: I don't understand why you should find it so objectionable.

SCOTT: The adjective "pretty" is for girls, or pretty boys of— ambiguous gender . . .

ZELDA: Girls, boys, whatever's pretty is pretty. Never mind ambiguity of—

SCOTT: In a man?

ZELDA: What? In a man?

SCOTT: Being called pretty implies—

ZELDA: Implies? What? —Implication?

SCOTT: A disparagement of—

ZELDA: What?

SCOTT: You know as well as I know that what it disparages is—
the virility of— [*He takes another drink.*]

ZELDA: Oh, but that's so established in your case. And even if
it wasn't—know what I think?

SCOTT: Never.

ZELDA: I think that to write well about women, there's got to
be that, a part of that, in the writer, oh, not too much, not so
much that he flits about like a—

SCOTT: Fairy?

ZELDA: You're too hard on them, Scott. I don't know why. Do
they keep chasing you because you're so pretty they think you
must be a secret one of them?

SCOTT: Zelda, quit this, it's downright mockery.

ZELDA: Don't take it seriously, it's just envy, Scott—I'm not
pretty at all.

SCOTT: Zelda, you know that you're an internationally celebrated beauty.

ZELDA: Oh? Am I?

SCOTT: The latest issue of *Cosmopolitan* magazine has a ship-
board photograph of us with Scotty, and the caption says—

ZELDA: Headed for an iceberg?

31

SCOTT: Says: "Brilliant young F. Scott Fitzgerald and his *beautiful* wife, Zelda, sail for France. *Bon voyage!*"

ZELDA: A slightly sinister—caption. Scott? Desperate can go with beauty, with an illusion of it.

SCOTT: —Desperate? —Are you desperate, Zelda?

[*Pause: music comes in at a low level. Zelda runs her hands tenderly through Scott's blond hair and along his face.*]

ZELDA [*looking darkly over his head*]: Have no right to be, but—

SCOTT: But you are? —Are you?

ZELDA: —You fall asleep first, before me.

SCOTT: Do I?

ZELDA: Yes. I hold you. I caress your smooth body, sleeping; then feel mine. —Mine's harder, not so delicate to the touch.

SCOTT: What are you telling me, Zelda? I'm not satisfactory to you? As a—

ZELDA: Sometimes I wish that the fires were equal.

SCOTT: Too much of mine goes to work, but—

ZELDA: —Work. —Loveliest of all four-letter words. . . . Circumstances such as—disparities—might some day—come between us. A little, or seem to—but this golden band on my finger's the truth. . . . [*She establishes the ring, removing it from her finger and slipping it on his.*] The lasting truth, even—whatever—time brings little divisions and you are better than me at the cover-up,

32

Scott. [*She opens a copy of the* Princeton Triangle Club.]
—Why didn't you ever show me this?

SCOTT: —*That?*

ZELDA: Is this really a picture of you?

[*A blowup of the picture appears on the drop behind the desk.*]

SCOTT: —Zelda, you know very well that every year the Princeton Triangle Club put on a show. Somebody had to appear as
the ingénue in it. —That year, I was chosen to play it. Yes, that's
me. What of it?

ZELDA: —Exquisite . . . a perfect illusion. I'd never achieve
it so well.

SCOTT: Who showed that to you? For what purpose?

ZELDA: A lady fan of your fiction—came up to me with it on
the beach today. —A gushy type, probably meant no harm but
was so loud, "Why, Mrs. Fitzgerald, Mrs. Scott Fitzgerald, can't
believe it, but they swear it's your husband! Surely not, but the
name is—" —Sara said, "Please! You're interrupting—"

SCOTT: Zelda, you are interrupting my work! Mustn't *do* that,
thought it was agreed you wouldn't!

ZELDA: What about my work?

SCOTT: Your—?

ZELDA: You're not going out tonight? —To the casino and the
masquerade?

SCOTT: Obviously not—since working!

33

ZELDA: Scott? Goofo? You need a night off to refresh you. You're driving yourself too hard.

SCOTT: That may be, but the purpose is—necessary. To live and live well. In keeping with our—

ZELDA: What?

SCOTT: Reputation!

ZELDA: Regardless of price? Scott, you're wearing yourself thin for something that I already suspect isn't worth it, at the price. We're on the *Cote d'Azur* with golden people. Generous to us. But the effort to match their bets at the casino, to run in their tracks is—too demanding of my nerves and your—liver . . .

SCOTT: What about my liver?

ZELDA: Dr. D'Amboise had a private talk with me.

SCOTT: About my—

ZELDA: Liver. He didn't want to alarm you but there is already some damage to it, and going on like this—the damage will be progressive. —*Oh! Widow's moon!*

SCOTT: What's a widow's moon?

ZELDA: Nearly full. When it's full the cherries will be ripe and when the cherries are ripe the nightingales stop singing. —Bearing the cherries home to their hungry little nestlings.

SCOTT: You seem to have picked up a lot of local lore. But, Zelda, regardless of my liver and the charms of the widow's moon, I do have to get on with my work. Did you hear me? I must GET ON WITH MY WORK!

ZELDA: What about mine, my work? —What sort of face are you making? Turn around, let me see!

[*Scott whirls about to face her. This short scene must catch the paradox of the love-hate relationship which existed between them at this point in their marriage.*]

Oh, that *is* quite a face! A face to strike terror to the heart of any person not equally savage. Well, there is equality in us there: savagery equal, both sides.

SCOTT: Zelda, we are *one* side, indivisible. You know that, by God, you'd better know that since I've staked my life on it, that you'd know it and accept it and—respect it!

[*His shaking hand seizes the glass; he drains it and then hurls it away.*]

ZELDA: Naughty, naughty young writer, drinking while working. So. One side, indivisible, created in liberty and justice with freedom for all? Ha, ha, paraphrase of the oath of allegiance to the classroom flag. So. Sit down. I only want a minute of your time.

SCOTT: I am not going to sit down again. I am standing to face you and hear you.

ZELDA: Hear me, good, a change. But answer me, this time, that would be a change, too. I want an answer to my first question, "What about *my* work?"

SCOTT: You are the wife of a highly respected and successful writer who works night and day to maintain you in—

ZELDA [*overlapping*]: An impossible situation? Oh, yes, you do that; I don't dispute your intense absorption in work. Yours!

35

I still say, "What about *mine*, meaning my *work*?"—Answer? None? —You threw the glass away, drink out of the bottle.

SCOTT [*throwing the bottle away*]: Your work is the work that all young Southern ladies dream of performing some day. Living well with a devoted husband and a beautiful child.

ZELDA: Are you certain, Scott, that I fit the classification of dreamy young Southern lady? Damn it, Scott. Sorry, wrong size, it pinches! —Can't wear that shoe, too confining.

SCOTT: I see. It's too confining. But it's all that we have in stock!

ZELDA: —Excuse my interruption. I'll not prolong it; I'll not do it again; I'll—find my own way somehow. Used to have some aptitude for dancing: could take that up again, or—I could betray you by taking a lover. . . . Could I? —I could give it a try . . .

[*Zelda exits into the asylum and is masked by the sisters who hold their positions till she returns. Scott exits at the rear of the stage. Two men enter from the same point and remove the table and chairs. Two dancers enter from either side of the stage for a* pas de deux *as the light changes into long, late afternoon shadows on a beach. Zelda reappears in a large, white straw hat and beach robe and sits on the rock, downstage. Edouard appears wearing the intern's jacket. The sisters mask him as he takes off the jacket and reappears in a swimsuit of the period. The dancers exit to the rear as Edouard moves down to Zelda on the rocks. He dries his head with a towel.*]

ZELDA: What a beautiful dive you made off the rocks. We call it a swan dive.

EDOUARD: I went very deep, so deep I nearly touched bottom.

ZELDA: You are reckless, you have a reckless nature and so have I!

EDOUARD: I know when to be careful: but do you?

ZELDA: I don't care to be careful! Anyway, we are alone!

EDOUARD: There could be hidden observers.

[*Zelda laughs and clasps his shining head between her hands and kisses him intensely.*]

Zelda, Zelda, your hands, please: the *plage* is public! You are—

ZELDA: Unnatural?

EDOUARD: Impulsive—dangerously—this is not the way of the French; we know passion but we also know caution. With public caution, our passions can be indulged in private. There must be the fictitious names on the register of the—

ZELDA: *Chambre de convenance!* You see, I've picked up the idiom for it in case, just in case—

EDOUARD: I know you've never used such a room before.

ZELDA: No, but how would you know?

EDOUARD: By intuition, Frenchmen have intuition.

ZELDA: And as for the fictitious name, mine I'd like to be Daisy.

EDOUARD: Why Daisy?

ZELDA: I was quite infatuated with the mysterious, dashing young Gatsby, and Daisy was his love: a wanton creature, not encumbered with morals, scruples, gifted with—how did Scott put it?—the enormous carelessness of the very rich.

EDOUARD: This is a matter to be approached seriously, Zelda.

ZELDA: Later, yes, not yet. If I approached the matter seriously now, at this moment, with you all wet and gleaming from your swan dive off the rocks, I think I'd cry—diamond tears.

EDOUARD: If serious precautions aren't taken about this—much as I want it to happen and to be altogether happy—we've got to recognize the gravity of the possibilities— In French I could say it easily; the words come right in French; our language was made for making arrangements of this kind—not so close. Can you look casual, Zelda, and listen? I think I know the little hotel. Fictitious names, yes, but not Daisy and not Gatsby, on the register. I'll use the names of my maternal grandparents!

ZELDA: Who were named?

EDOUARD: Better that you don't know them, you'd blab them out at some—hysterical moment.

ZELDA: It's probably not Southern-lady-like to have secrets which are held sacred but—I shall have one, a secret kept securely. I've turned away from you; I've picked up a shell, coiled, iridescent—an innocent occupation for possible observers while we complete our plans for the illicit occasion in private. Behind a locked door, a securely locked door?

EDOUARD: A door that's locked and bolted.

ZELDA: With a window facing the sea, open, to admit the sea-wind and the wave sounds, but with curtains that blow inward as if wanting to participate in our caresses! —Here's another, shell, not coiled, but—the window not so high that we'd break bones if we had to escape that way, the door being stormed by—

EDOUARD: You're trembling, Zelda. Are you cold?

ZELDA: *Au contraire.*

EDOUARD: Frightened?

ZELDA: God, no! Are *you?*

EDOUARD: A bit shocked by the—imprudence.

ZELDA: But not repelled? Not wanting to call it off?

EDOUARD: *Non, non au contraire.* —Shells, birds, creatures of sea and sky . . .

ZELDA: You'll have your security measures, *cher*, locked, bolted door, but behind closed curtains there must be light in the room, you must be all visible to me, indelibly—*im-mem-orially!*—in my heart's eye, if this adventure blows out the eye of the mind. So? When? Tomorrow? *Demain?*

EDOUARD: At noon, tomorrow, here, *sur la plage.* We'll swim a ways up to the pier. I'll have a taxi waiting to take us to a little *auberge*—the *Reve Bleu.*

ZELDA: Promise? Sacred as secret?

EDOUARD: *D'accord, d'accord, entendu!*

ZELDA: *Merci mille fois!*

EDOUARD: A beautiful girl does not thank a man for enjoying

39

intimacy with her. —We're being observed by a woman with binoculars on the *plage*.

ZELDA [*loudly, almost shouting*]: How many shells have we collected.

EDOUARD: Only these two.

ZELDA: Two will be sufficient for our purpose at the *Auberge Reve Bleu*.

EDOUARD: How strange and lovely you are . . .

[*The dancers reappear and as soon as they have reached center-stage, Edouard exits into the asylum. Zelda remains seated on the floor while the* pas de deux *continues upstage of her.*]

ZELDA [*to herself*]: And so the appointment is made! The hawk and the hawk will meet in light near the sun!

[*Zelda stretches out onto the floor in her spotlight while the love* pas de deux *finishes as the curtain comes down.*]

END OF ACT I

ACT TWO

SCENE ONE

*The scene opens with the sound of wind sweeping the hilltop:
as if a dark cloud had blown over it, the asylum lawn is dimmed
out.*

*The little hotel room is set up downstage of the flaming bush.
There is a double bed with an arched headboard and two chairs,
one on either side of the bed.*

*On the chair to the left of the bed are Edouard's jacket, shirt,
and pants—also his wallet with a photograph, an ash tray, and a
pack of cigarettes and matches.*

*On the chair to the right of the bed are Zelda's dress, a bottle
of opened champagne, and two glasses. Her shoes are near the
chair.*

*The light is brought up, cool, as if the light of a full moon
shone through the shutters.*

*Edouard and Zelda (in her younger guise) are visible, nude
except for whatever conventions of stage propriety may be in
order.*

ZELDA: The little hotel has such an appropriate name.

EDOUARD: *Reve Bleu. C'est àpropos. Vraiment.* How do you
feel, Zelda?

ZELDA: Innocent, quite innocent. A lunatic is innocent until
proven sane.

EDOUARD: *C'est lui, je crois.*

ZELDA: Meaning who?

41

EDOUARD: I believe it is your husband.

ZELDA: Oh. My very late husband. Is he pacing the garden?

EDOUARD: *Non. Il est assis.*

ZELDA: When you forget me, you speak in French. Where is he seated?

EDOUARD: *Sur la*—excuse me, on the bench.

ZELDA: How like him, how terribly like him, patiently seated outside while his wife and heroine of his fiction betrays him upstairs.

EDOUARD: I made sure that no one would be admitted. I heard loud voices downstairs—while you were crying out so wildly during your—

ZELDA: Creating a drunken disturbance was he? Sometimes I think his whole life has been a drunken disturbance, except—

EDOUARD: I believe he suspects. I think he knows. And the American husband takes a slight infidelity on the part of his wife very seriously, it appears, from the look on his face.

ZELDA: Slight, did you say? A slight infidelity, was it? Scott and I always made love in silence. Tonight was the one time that I cried out wildly. But, oh, how quiet you were: strong, enormously, and assured, completely, but not—not impassioned. Of course, your adventures of this kind are many and probably varied—mine, this once. . . . And I think never again . . .

EDOUARD: I think he knows but he cannot be certain until we leave the hotel, if he continues to wait that long on the bench.

42

ZELDA: He must fly back to the Coast where he has a new love of his own.

EDOUARD: Shhh.

ZELDA: The champagne is still cool as the counterfeit moon, and I am cold without you. Return. Come back to the bed. We haven't slept together, only made love. These are words. Words are the love acts of writers. Don't turn. I love your back. It's sculptured by Praxiteles and even in the moon wash, it's copper gleaming. Except for the groin which is dark with imagination . . .

EDOUARD: You found me unusually quiet?

ZELDA: No, no, he is quiet, too. Even his work is never loud with passion. It is controlled—desperately. Very beautifully, often . . . sometimes classic . . .

EDOUARD: I had to be controlled, and I had to be quiet. He may have recognized your cries.

ZELDA: How could he, having never heard them before? I am out of bed; I am on my feet, approaching you. . . . No, don't turn. I want to flatten my body against your back.

EDOUARD: *Pas si fort, la voix.*

ZELDA: But if he knows, he knows. Throw the shutters open and cry out, "I have taken your wife!"

EDOUARD: Just be quiet, and he will have no proof.

ZELDA [*shouting through the shutters*]: The flyer has taken me from you! You do not respond, Edouard.

EDOUARD: Response is for the living. And passion, too.

ZELDA: I felt even your memory with passion.

EDOUARD: I am an aviator, you know, and for those of my calling which is flight in the sky—that is true passion and it will always take me away.

ZELDA: I know. For better or worse. I know that I must resume the part created for me. Mrs. F. Scott Fitzgerald. Without that part, would I have ever been known, except as a woman who cried out wildly in the arms of a man married to the sky? Did I love Scott? Belonging to, is it love? *Ça depend.* If he makes of me a monument with his carefully arranged words, is that my life, my recompense for madness? There is none. Have you nothing to leave me when you've flown? In terror of this beautiful indiscretion between us?

EDOUARD: I have this photograph.

[*She takes it. There is a pause.*]

ZELDA: All photographs are a poor likeness and so are paintings; they don't have the warmth of the living flesh so loved, nor even the warmth of the memory of it. You want to go. Leaving a poor photograph of you. Photographs contain no likeness of heads gold as Christmas coins, or bronze hands cupping the breast, cupping the groin and the thighs, as if to engrave remembrance after madness and death.

EDOUARD: I think it may be possible to dissolve, to leave unnoticed. Strange things are occurring tonight. There's a magic about it. I see it in the sky, I hear it in the wind. [*A birdcall is heard.*] *Un rossignol.* [*He lifts his face to the sky.*] *Oui, je reviens!*

44

ZELDA: I know what you said, you said that you were returning; you said it to the sky and the bird, not to me.

[*Dance music of the twenties fades in.*]

EDOUARD: Music—the party's started.

ZELDA: Here? At the hotel *Reve Bleu*?

EDOUARD: At the Murphy's dance. We're expected. *Non—non!* —Child of Alabama . . . we must arrive on time to avoid suspicion.

ZELDA [*dressing rapidly*]: Into my party dress, and you—

EDOUARD: Into my dress uniform. What a lovely dress for the party.

ZELDA: A whisper of cerise chiffon. And under? Nothing! Remember? We danced at the edge of the light and we danced as if lovemaking. . . . You know I expected our affair to continue, no matter what it might cost.

EDOUARD: Could I have saved you, Zelda? We must arrive separately so I'll leave first.

ZELDA: *Attends, un moment de plus!* —Why they've removed our room! Our little hotel!

EDOUARD: A dream dissolves that way.

ZELDA: But it wasn't a dream. It happened.

EDOUARD: Once, yes. But now? —Don't claw my shoulders! I'd have to explain it in the barracks tonight.

45

[*They exit to the rear. There is a medley of indistinct voices, animated and gay, voices of people gathering for a party. The asylum lawn is lighted again, strewn with lanterns, and party guests in evening dress are seen dancing. Edouard enters from the rear of the stage and makes his way through the dancing couples. He moves downstage near the rocks. Zelda enters seconds later from the rear and wanders between the rocks and the downstage end of the bench, making her way through the party guests, following Edouard.*]

ZELDA [*to Edouard*]: Why—hello! —It's so long since I've seen you that I thought you were gone for good, but you've dropped by for the Murphy's party?

EDOUARD: No, not really for that. I have only dropped by to thank you for an unearthly adventure and to wish you—no regrets. How lovely you are in that *robe-de-soir* with the—ruby necklace . . .

ZELDA: I have no rubies. Wives of writers, even eminent writers, well-paid by the *Saturday Evening Post*—are not decked out with many precious stones; no, these were loaned me by Sara Murphy for this—bizarre occasion. Some people were so kind, and afterwards it's the kindness you remember, the rest is trivia, dissolved, dropped away . . .

EDOUARD: How lovely you are in that—

ZELDA: You said that before.

EDOUARD: Have you no photograph for *me*?

ZELDA: You want it back? The one of you that you gave me?

EDOUARD: I meant one of you, dear savage.

ZELDA: I would have to inscribe it and I'm afraid the inscription would be embarrassingly candid for a gentleman-flyer so attached to convention.

EDOUARD: I would not expose it to anyone but myself in private at night.

ZELDA: Privacy? In a barracks? —I am going to return your photograph to you. I am careless with things. I would be likely to leave it on my bedside table, that's how careless I am with Caesar's things. Here. Take it back, I don't need it. Don't want it. Photographs are a *petit souvenir* but not a good likeness at all. They can't penetrate the flesh, they have no heart, no fury, no explosion of molten—I was about to say fire, oh, God, about to say to you fire, that element you crashed in! Didn't you, later on, love?

[*Edouard gently disengages himself from Zelda's hands.*]

EDOUARD: —No, I—

ZELDA: I was certain that eventually you and that plane, in which you performed aerial acrobatics over the red-tiled roof of the Villa Marie, would crash in fire.

EDOUARD: I must disappoint you. Nothing like that happened to me at all.

ZELDA: Then what did happen to you? After you left me that summer?

EDOUARD: Well, gradually, as such things occur to most living creatures, Zelda, I—*grew old* . . .

ZELDA: No, not to you, that is not permitted! *C'est défendu! C'est impossible pour toi!*

47

EDOUARD: You're too romantic. I did grow old—weighted down with honors. *Grand-croix de la Légion d'honneur, Croix de guerre,* and finally—*Grand-croix au Mérite de l'ordre de Malte* . . .

ZELDA: So many impressive honors! I never knew. My congratulations if not too long delayed?

EDOUARD: I'm afraid that that sort of thing—public esteem, orders of merit—are what we must live for.

ZELDA: The only respected alternative to descent in flame.

EDOUARD: Little Alabama, your head's still full of "huge, cloudy symbols of high romance." They—dissolve, too. —Hold onto your benefits, Zelda.

ZELDA: Such as what? I'm glad I was spared the sight of your gentle decline into age. . . . I'm sure you managed it with as much grace as could be hoped for. Now say something gallant to *me*.

EDOUARD: You were—you are—radiant with beauty.

ZELDA: Tonight at that trick of a hotel called *Reve Bleu,* I thought I was holding your body against me inseparably close, so tight that I felt the blades of your bones carved to mine. You were bronze gold; you smelled of the sand and the sun (on a bed cooled by a Mediterranean moon). Yes, I felt you underneath starched linen. I think I frightened you a little. Is it bad of a woman, I mean a well-bred Southern lady, not a professional *putain,* to be sensual?

EDOUARD: No, but—

ZELDA: I think Scott feels it is; he thinks a woman's love should be delicate as a fairy-tale romance. I don't think he's ever looked deeply enough into my eyes. If he did I wouldn't serve so well as the heroine of his fiction. But you're an aviator; you dare the sky. But I think even you are a little frightened of—

EDOUARD: Of such intensity, yes. A Frenchman has a male conceit that makes him prefer to be dominant in love. Zelda, I must go back to quarters at Fréjus, now.

ZELDA: Away to grow old and weighted down with honors, *Croix de*—everything but—*Calvary's Christ?*

EDOUARD: We must hold our benefits, Zelda, make much of them, a life.

ZELDA: Of what? For me? A flame burning nothing? Not even casting a shadow? A match for a cigarette does better than that. Look. Edouard? I'll ask Scott for my freedom if you'll have me!

EDOUARD: Careful, careful, hold on to what's secure.

ZELDA: I'd be quite willing to perform the act of love with you at the height of a cloudless noon, on top of the *Arc de triomphe*, enormously magnified for all of Paris, all the *world* to see.

EDOUARD: That sketch of a room with shutters served us better.

ZELDA [*with a touch of bitterness, now*]: How dearly you do value discretion! *Is it worth it?* You're looking around, you're looking this way and that way! [*She is approaching a kind of fury at his concern for what she regards as inconsequential values.*] *Is there a woman with binoculars in the bushes?* Is the *secret* called *truth* being overheard by someone or everyone that's hostile to it? My benefits, are they *discretions*, are they deceptions?

EDOUARD: Zelda, please, we mustn't create a *scandale*.

ZELDA: I think you mean, *"Don't live!"* —Well—I didn't want to when you'd gone. And I think you ought to know this because someday you may wear it on your dress uniform with your other decorations. After you'd gone back to the sky, I did this in honor of my love for you—I swallowed all the contents of a bottle of narcotics!

EDOUARD: Zelda! Hush!

ZELDA: And Sara Murphy walked me up and down the bedroom to keep me from falling asleep for always, alll-wayyys!

[*The passion of her cry makes Edouard clap a hand to her mouth. She twists violently for a moment; then her fury passed, she leans against his shoulder.*]

EDOUARD: *Pourquoi?* Why did you?

ZELDA: The only message I ever thought I had was four pirouettes and a *fouetté*, and—it turned out to be about as cryptic as a Chinese laundry ticket . . . but the will to cry out remains. The orchestra's playing a tango. Please, please—take me to the dance floor?

[*Zelda leads Edouard toward the music; they exit to the rear as Scott enters from the asylum doors—as he appeared much younger—and rushes onto the lawn. He gasps, covers his face, and sways.*]

MURPHY: Has he seen them together, Zelda and the flyer?

SCOTT: My God, Gilbert Seldes just called out to me from his balcony next to ours.

MURPHY: Called out what?

SCOTT [*in a choked voice*]: That Joseph Conrad just died.

MURPHY [*insufficiently moved or surprised*]: Really?

SCOTT [*mocking his unemotional tone*]: "Really?"

MRS. PATRICK CAMPBELL: My dear young man, to a party one brings the latest fashions and gossip, not obituaries.

SCOTT [*turning to her furiously*]: What you bring to a party is a fading reputation and a double chin.

MURPHY: Eventually we all bring that to parties, if we're still invited to parties. And being offensive to ladies doesn't increase your popularity at them. You've insulted a friend of ours: apologize to her, Scott.

MRS. PATRICK CAMPBELL: No, no, no, I haven't been insulted in much too long!

SCOTT: You amaze me, all of you amaze me! I bring you word that Joseph Conrad's just died and you go right on—what are you doing? Setting up a Maypole? If I had known that this was a children's party, I'd have brought Scotty. Set up a Maypole in honor of Conrad's death.

SARA: I must have missed something. What is it?

SCOTT: Gilbert Seldes—

SARA: Oh, Gilbert Seldes! Did we forget to ask him?

SCOTT: Sara, I said that Gilbert Seldes has just shouted to me

51

from the balcony next to ours that Conrad has just died. We've lost our only writer with a great tragic sense.

MRS. PATRICK CAMPBELL: Oh, that's why I found him so difficult to read!

SCOTT: May I—may I have a drink?

SARA: Was that your reply?

SCOTT: No, that's my need at the moment.

MURPHY: Scott, will you please hold it down tonight?

SCOTT: Hold down what? —The shock of being informed of Joseph Conrad's death?

SARA: Yes, of course, but please don't talk about death at a dance and please don't smash Venetian goblets or Baccarat crystal.

SCOTT: Okay, *touché*. —Is Zelda here?

[*Tango music begins.*]

SARA: Yes, and I asked her, "Where's Scott?" —She said, "Oh, working—working."

[*Zelda and Edouard appear dancing the tango. They move centerstage and then exit opposite.*]

—She's lost when you're lost in work, and it's difficult for her, you know.

SCOTT: I know. She's jealous of it. Well, she has her French aviator and swimming and nude sunbathing on the rocks, probably not alone.

SARA: It's just an innocent little flirtation, Scott.

SCOTT: There they are dancing together. Does it look innocent to you?

SARA: The tango isn't supposed to look like a Quaker square dance! That elegant new nigra we enticed from the Moulin Rouge is going to sing.

SCOTT: It's disgraceful. It's got to be stopped! Something's got to be done. Something's—Doctor—

[*Scott seems abruptly confused. The light changes. The party guests exit left and right and Dr. Zeller enters from the doors of the asylum. He approaches Scott.*]

Dr., uh—Bleumer . . .

DR. ZELLER: I am Dr. Zeller.

SCOTT: May I talk to Dr. Bleumer with whom I talked by phone from the Coast this morning?

DR. ZELLER: Mr. Fitzgerald, I think you must be confused.

SCOTT: I regard that as an impertinent remark. When I say that I talked to Dr. Bleumer this morning—

DR. ZELLER: It's not an unnatural confusion.

SCOTT: Dr. Bleumer assured me that Zelda's condition was much improved, that she was enjoying such a long and encouraging state of remission that it might soon be possible to release her.

DR. ZELLER: I've heard of Dr. Bleumer but—I'm sorry, he's never been on our staff. I say that it's a natural confusion because we have your wife's complete history, of course, and she's been a patient of sanitariums in Switzerland where Dr. Bleumer practiced.

SCOTT: God damn it, whoever talked to me, called me here from the Coast, did assure me I'd find her transformed, so I caught the first plane out without stopping for suitable clothes. And look down there! Do you recognize that overblown middle-aged woman down there?

DR. ZELLER: Mr. Fitzgerald, I would not have recognized you from the photograph on the dust jacket of *The Great Gatsby*.

SCOTT: Taken sixteen years ago, *Gatsby* was published sixteen years ago, before that pathetic creature—turned me to this middle-aged—robbed me of my—

DR. ZELLER: Youth, were you going to say youth?

SCOTT: —I don't say—obvious things. If you know my work you should know—I never write or say—obvious—things . . .
[*Dr. Zeller, having observed Scott's shaken condition, places a supportive arm about Scott's shoulder.*]

Take your arm off me! I don't like being touched by men!

DR. ZELLER: Mr. Fitzgerald, you were about to fall.

[*The word "fall" is repeated as if an echo was fading into the wind.*]

SCOTT: Yes—sometimes—nearly. —Zelda is with a young man down there, behaving with no regard for the public appearance of it.

DR. ZELLER: Oh, yes. —One of our young interns is with her.

SCOTT: She calls him by the name of a young French aviator with whom she had an affair in the south of France. She calls him, "Edouard—Edouard!"

DR. ZELLER: Yes, well—Mr. Fitzgerald, we've found it a privilege to treat your wife Zelda for her own sake, not just because she's your wife. It's lucky we've had this meeting. I like to read important writing, and I feel that your wife's novel *Save Me the Waltz*—I'm sure you won't mind my saying that there are passages in it that have a lyrical imagery that moves me, sometimes, more than your own.

SCOTT: My publishers and I edited that book! —Tried to make it coherent.

DR. ZELLER: I'm not deprecating your work; I wouldn't think of deprecating your work, but I stand by my belief that—

SCOTT: That none of my—desperately—well-ordered—understood writing is equal to the—

DR. ZELLER: More desperately—somehow controlled—in spite of the—

SCOTT: Madness . . .

DR. ZELLER: All right. —Mr. Fitzgerald, I think you suspect as well as I know that Zelda has sometimes struck a sort of fire in her work that—I'm sorry to say this to you, but I never quite found anything in yours, even yours, that was—equal to it . . .

[*Scott sways and uses the bench for support.*]

Sisters! —Take Mr. Fitzgerald inside; he should have a little sedation—a little something to calm him.

SCOTT: No, no, angina again. I'll take a nitro tablet and just rest a bit.

[*The lights change. The scene returns to the party and music begins. The Hemingways are arriving. They enter from upstage left and move centerstage behind the pavilion ribbons.*]

SARA: Hadley! Hem!

MURPHY: What do you think, Ernest?

HEMINGWAY: About what, Gerry?

MURPHY: Zelda's infatuation with the handsome young French aviator? Innocent or not?

HEMINGWAY: Zelda's a crazy, Scott's a rummy, so speculation is useless and interest is wasted.

MURPHY: She's wandering among us as if completely alone.

HEMINGWAY: The solitude of the lunatic is never broken by no matter what number.

SARA [*calling out*]: Zelda!

ZELDA [*calls softly*]: Edouard?

HEMINGWAY: Surrounded by thousands, she'd still be completely alone.

SARA: Do you think that Scott's alcoholism is driving Zelda mad, or is Zelda's madness driving Scott to alcoholism?

56

HEMINGWAY: Scott has talent: delicate sensibilities for a male writer—

MURPHY: You do allow him a certain talent, Ernest?

HADLEY: Scott's pushing Ernest's work harder than he pushes his own.

[*Zelda has come through the ribbons of the pavilion and moves behind/between Murphy and Hemingway.*]

ZELDA: —Why? [*Zelda steps back and continues to move to the right before turning to the group.*] I said, "Why?" Didn't anyone hear me? Is it the attraction of Ernest's invulnerable, virile nature? Isn't that the implication, that Scott is magnetized, infatuated with Ernest's somewhat too carefully cultivated aura of the prizefight and the bullring and the man-to-man attitude acquired from Gertrude Stein?

HEMINGWAY: I'm acquainted with the other side of the coin. The excessive praise on the one side and the—envious other. I will go on: strong—oh, will accept convenient introductions but don't need them. My work will be hard and disciplined till it stops. Then—quit by choice—and rich . . . but—

HADLEY: Will I still be your girl?

HEMINGWAY: Be good.

HADLEY: You mean devoutly devoted to you, even when discarded for the next?

[*The elegant black entertainer has started singing a haunting song of the period, offstage left. He hums as he enters upstage of the pavilion and sings as he moves to the opening of the pavilion.*]

Who's that *exotic* young man singing my favorite song?

MURPHY: The latest sensation of the Moulin Rouge.

SARA: We flew him down for our party.

[*Zelda has seated herself on the rock, downstage. Sara watches her and then joins her on the rock. The singer sings through-out the following dialogue.*]

Zelda, are you looking for someone?

ZELDA: I was with Edouard. Where is he? Where's he gone?

SARA: Why, he just said good night, had to get back to—his barracks.

ZELDA: Edouard's left me *alone* here?

SARA: Zelda, you're not alone here.

ZELDA: I'm afraid so, Sara—I have no gift for friendship.

SARA: I meant Scott.

ZELDA: What about Scott?

SARA: He's arrived at the party.

ZELDA: Do you think Scott's arrival means that I'm not alone?

[*The song ends.*]

SARA: He's had a shock—someone's death.

[*The singer exits stage right.*]

I'm not sure who it was. [*She lowers her voice.*] Please be careful, Zelda!

ZELDA: Are you warning me not to make a remark on the tip of my tongue? —A remark that would violate the rules of the game? Well. I'm not sure that I could ever be intimidated by rules into sticking quite faithfully to them, especially when abandoned by—the young man with whom I've committed my first infidelity to Scott, a young man to whom I'd offered myself as mistress in preference to continuing my shadow of an existence as Mrs.— Eminent Author . . .

[*Scott abruptly confronts Zelda, shaking her.*]

SCOTT: Hush, hush! Privately. I knew! Here we're in public!

ZELDA: The young man declined. "Hold on to your benefits," he warned me, and then I think my heart died and I—went—mad.

[*Overlap.*]

[*Scott claps his hand over Zelda's mouth. She bites him.*]

SCOTT: Christ, you bit my hand. She bit my— Most men would have struck you down for what you've announced at this—

HEMINGWAY: Scott had better have a rabies shot.

[*Hemingway laughs loudly, coarsely drunk.*]

SARA: Ernest, don't! We must all try to smooth this over or the party will be spoiled, and it's such a lovely party, probably the last party this season.

[*The dance music begins again. The singer and an extremely*

59

thin woman with a lovely face, in a twenties evening gown, enter from upstage left and dance their way to downstage right.]

MURPHY: Sara, darling, your wonderful black singer is dancing now.

MRS. PATRICK CAMPBELL: And what is that?

SARA: Did you say what or who?

MRS. PATRICK CAMPBELL: Whichever suits the case.

SARA: The singer or the dancer?

MRS. PATRICK CAMPBELL: They both appear to be dancing and in a highly provocative fashion.

SARA: He is the latest craze of Paris. Appears at the Moulin Rouge.

MRS. PATRICK CAMPBELL: And she? Of the scarcely tangible physique?

[*The dancers have made their exit.*]

SARA: Anorexia nervosa.

MRS. PATRICK CAMPBELL: Ah, you know everybody. —Would he do an apache dance with me? I've always wanted to do an apache dance, not a violent one, but—*adagio* . . .

SARA: He's very accommodating, but if I ask him, will you tell me if this is a true or apocryphal story about an adventure of yours in Hollywood?

MRS. PATRICK CAMPBELL: Very few stories about me are too outrageous to be true, or even outrageous enough. Which one is this?

SARA: That your poodle relieved his bowels in a cab and when you arrived at your destination, the cabdriver discovered what had occurred and made a scene about it in vulgar language. And you said, "It wasn't my dog—it was me."

MRS. PATRICK CAMPBELL: Even if it weren't true would I disown such an hilarious anecdote as that? And now, the apache dance?

[*There is a reprise of the song.*]

SARA: Soon as he's finished.

[*The singer begins to hum offstage.*]

MRS. PATRICK CAMPBELL: What a rare and lovely party this is: are all of us—you know what?

SARA: I'll have to check the guest list.

MRS. PATRICK CAMPBELL: Surely nothing comparable to it before. Why, there's Scott, again.

SARA: Whenever he approaches Ernest I alert the waiters to prepare for a disturbance.

MRS. PATRICK CAMPBELL: —Yes . . .

SARA: What?

MRS. PATRICK CAMPBELL: I just said, "Yes"—I've said wittier things but none so appropriate to an occasion of unlimited license.

61

Death is that: and after many outraged cries of "no," well, it's finally, "yes" and "yes" and "yes" . . .

[*The singer has entered from the right and now begins to sing "Sophisticated Lady" softly as he moves to the opening of the pavilion. Scott crosses to Hemingway.*]

SCOTT: What's that milk-choc'late fairy know about sophisticated ladies?

HEMINGWAY: Why don't you ask him, Scott, go right on up and ask him.

SCOTT: Think I'm scared to?

HEMINGWAY: You're not drunk enough yet.

SCOTT: Watch this! [*Scott approaches the singer.*] HEY! MILK-CHOC'LATE, WANTA ASK YOU SOMETHING! Which gender do you prefer?

[*The singer springs at Scott and flattens him with one blow; then he exits stage right. Sara goes to Murphy.*]

SARA: How did it happen?

MURPHY: Hemingway put him up to it.

SARA: We must never have them together at a party. [*She raises her voice.*] A buffet's being served in the pavilion, if anybody's interested in supper.

MRS. PATRICK CAMPBELL: Do I smell bouillabaisse?

[*The party drifts into the pavilion.*]

HEMINGWAY: Old bitches never die, just smell bouillabaisse.

[*Scott rises. Hemingway crosses to a waiter who is holding a tray of drinks.*]

The ladies and gentlemen seem to have left us alone together. For what? A *mano-mano*?

[*Scott looks bewildered.*]

Oh, but you're not acquainted with the idioms of the bullring.

SCOTT: I'm afraid they're mostly meaningless to me, Hem.

HEMINGWAY [*handing him a drink*]: *À chacun sa merde!* Careful don't spill.

SCOTT: A damaged ticker makes you shaky sometimes, even after a—nitro . . .

HEMINGWAY: I suppose it makes it difficult for you to sleep—always wondering if you'll ever wake up. But you were always a light sleeper. I remember that trip to Lyon to pick up your topless Renault from a repair shop—you had a sleepless night when the rain stopped us on the way back.

SCOTT: A bitch of a cold.

HEMINGWAY: You had a cold—oh, yes . . . [*He is restless, paces.*] Scott, I've always had a feeling that it's a mistake for writers to know each other. The competitive element in the normal male nature is especially prominent in the nature of writers.

SCOTT: With so much in common? As you and I?

63

HEMINGWAY: A profession—only.

SCOTT: Not sensibilities?

HEMINGWAY: Yours and mine are totally different, Scott.

SCOTT: And yet—it's said of us both that we always write of the same woman, you of Lady Brett Ashley in various guises and me of—

HEMINGWAY: Zelda and Zelda and more Zelda. As if you'd like to appropriate her identity and her—

SCOTT: And her?

HEMINGWAY: Sorry, Scott, but I almost said—gender. That wouldn't have been fair. It's often been observed that duality of gender can serve some writers well.

[*He approaches Scott. For a moment we see their true depth of pure feeling for each other. Hemingway is frightened of it, however.*]

—Yes, some—to create equally good male and—

SCOTT: You are fortunate in having such an inexhaustibly interesting and complex nature, Hem, that regardless of how often you portray yourself in a book—

HEMINGWAY: Don't be a bitch. Where's the resemblance between Colonel Cantwell of *Across the River and into the Trees* and, say, the wounded American deserter from the Italian army in *Farewell to Arms*?

SCOTT: I don't recall the Colonel but I've no doubt he's one of your many and always fascinating self-portraits.

HEMINGWAY: Fuck it! —You know as well as I know that every goddam character an honest writer creates is part of himself. Don't you? —Well, *don't* you?

SCOTT: We do have multiple selves as well as what you call dual genders. —Hem? Let's admit we're—

HEMINGWAY: What?

SCOTT: Friends, Hem—true and very deep friends. You brought up the trip to Lyon for the topless Renault, which was topless because Zelda hated tops on cars.

HEMINGWAY: In all weather?

SCOTT: Hem, you never understood Zelda, not as much as me.

HEMINGWAY: Not as much as *you* understood Zelda?

SCOTT: I didn't understand Zelda either, no, I know that, now, but I loved her.

HEMINGWAY: And hated her, enemy, lover, same same, as the Chinaman says.

SCOTT: You just hated her and blamed her for my drinking and there was a double reason for that, you know. You wanted to believe that I had only one great book in me, *Gatsby*, that Zelda and drinking would preclude the possibility of anything to equal *Gatsby*—after . . .

HEMINGWAY: Which you attribute to professional envy, Scott?

SCOTT: More to the fact that I saved *The Sun Also Rises* from starting with the entire past history of Lady Brett Ashley, a thing that would have—

65

HEMINGWAY: If my own critical faculty hadn't been capable of— there was Maxwell Perkins—

SCOTT: To whom I'd introduced you. But, Hem, admit this much. You could *not* admit, then that anybody gave you professional help.

HEMINGWAY: Don't admit the truth of anyone's—cherished— illusions. Oh, hell, believe whatever's a comfort to you, believe it, but don't ask me to confirm the imagined truth of it, I don't offer that kind of comfort.

SCOTT: Ernest, you've always been able to be kind as well as cruel. Why, that night when I was so sick in Lyon—

HEMINGWAY: Not Lyon, *after* Lyon, at Chalon-sur—

SCOTT: Wherever's—no matter. I was catching pneumonia. You cared for me with the tenderness of—

HEMINGWAY [*cutting in quickly*]: The night? —Scott? You had the skin of a girl, mouth of a girl, the soft eyes of a girl, you— you solicited attention. I gave it, yes, I found you touchingly vulnerable.

SCOTT: These attributes, if I did have them in—

HEMINGWAY: You did have them.

SCOTT: And they were—repellent to you?

HEMINGWAY: They were disturbing to me.

SCOTT: Why?

HEMINGWAY: I'd rather not examine the reason too closely. Wouldn't you? Rather not?

scott: In privacy, under such special circumstances, why not, I don't see why not?

hemingway: You were so innocent, so guileless, Scott. Did you ever grow up? I don't mean older, but up. —Well? Can't you say?

scott: I'm trying to recall a certain short story of yours. The title doesn't come back to me right now but the story does. An Italian officer has been removed from any contact with women for weeks or months in some snowbound Alpine encampment during the war, the First. He has a young orderly waiting on him, a boy with the sort of androgynous appeal that you said I had in wherever after Lyon. —At last he asks the boy if he's engaged. The boy says he is married. He says it blushing, avoiding the officer's eyes, and goes out quickly. The officer wonders—significantly—if the boy was lying about it.

hemingway: I've also written a story called "Sea Change" about a couple, young man and older young man, on a ship sailing to Europe and—at first the younger man is shocked, or pretends to be shocked, by the older one's—attentions at night. However the sea change occurs and by the end of the voyage, the protesting one is more than reconciled to his patron's attentions. Look, Scott, it's my profession to observe and interpret all kinds of human relations. That's what serious writers hire out to do. Maybe it's rough, this commitment, but we honor it with truth as we observe and interpret it. And some day, I'll certainly write about a man not me, or at all related to me. He'll be completely you, Scott. In it, aspects, embarrassing aspects of you, will be suggested clearly to the knowledgeable reader. You see, I can betray even my oldest close friend, the one most helpful in the beginning. That may have been at least partly the reason for which I executed myself not long after, first by attempting to walk into the propeller of a plane—that having failed, by blasting my exhausted brains out with an elephant gun. Yes, I may have pronounced on myself this violent death sentence to expiate the betrayals I've strewn behind me in my solitary, all but totally solitary—

[*Pause. Hemingway turns from Scott and faces the audience with cold, hard pride.*]

There I stop it, this game. Would never appeal for sympathy with such a confession containing the word "solitary" which I never was. —*Was I?* [*Obviously he is not convinced of the matter.*] *WAS I?*

[*Scott faces him.*]

SCOTT: Ernest, you may regret that you asked for an answer to that. Do you want an answer to that?

HEMINGWAY: If you've got one to give me.

SCOTT: I suspect that you were lonelier than I and possibly you were even as lonely as Zelda.

[*They stare at each other.*]

HEMINGWAY: *Fuck it! Hadley, Hadley, call me, the game's gone soft, can't play it any longer!* [*Offstage, a woman's voice sings "Ma bionda."*]—That's Miss Mary whom you never knew, a good, loving friend, and a hunting, fishing companion—at the end. We sang that song together the night before I chose to blast my brains out for no reason but the good and sufficient reason that my work was finished, strong, hard work, all done—no reason for me to continue. . . . What do you make of that, Scott?

[*He hoarsely joins in Miss Mary's song as he crosses off, roughly brushing aside the delicate silk ribbons of the pavilion drop. Pause.*]

SCOTT: Zelda? —Zelda?

FADE OUT

SCENE TWO

We are back in the time and place of the play's beginnings. Shadows are long on the front lawn of Highland Hospital as sunset approaches. Scott is seated as at the end of the preceding scene, on the bench near the flaming bush.

Nuns flank the entrance. They slowly lift their arms so that their batwing sleeves mask Zelda's costume change. Scott rises unsteadily and looks incredulously about him at the spectral scene. Low clouds scudding over are projected on the "cyc." Shreds of vapor drift across the proscenium. There is a fragile and elegiac music of the sort that Prokofiev or Stravinsky might have composed. It fades out as the sisters slowly lower their masking sleeves from the entrance, disclosing Zelda as she appeared in the first scene of the play.

ZELDA [*to Sister One*]: Is he still waiting out there to say good-bye, as late and cold as this, in such unseasonable clothes?

[*Edouard appears behind her in the white jacket of the intern.*]

INTERN: Be kind. He's a gentleman and an artist.

ZELDA: Fatal combination.

INTERN: Now, yes: he died for attempting to exist as both. And so be kind to him, Zelda.

SCOTT [*calling*]: Zelda?

ZELDA: Of course I will be kind as possible to him.

INTERN: Offer him a sort of last sacrament. You know what I mean. "Drink this in remembrance of me whose blood was shed for thee to give thee—"

69

ZELDA: The Everlasting ticket that doesn't exist. The lies of Christ were such beautiful lies, especially on the night before crucifixion on The Place of the Skull.

INTERN: His disciples said that he rose again from the dead.

ZELDA: And ascended to the lawn of Highland Hospital.

SCOTT: Zelda?

ZELDA [*to the intern*]: I'll see you again before this occasion is over?

INTERN: Yes.

[*Zelda advances slowly toward Scott.*]

ZELDA: —I'm approaching him now, no son of God but a gentleman shadow of him. It's incredible how, against appalling odds, dear Scott achieved a Christly parallel through his honoring of long commitments, even now to me, a savage ghost in a bedraggled tutu, yes, it's a true and incredible thing.

SCOTT [*softly, as he falls back onto the bench*]: Incredible? —Yes.

[*She pauses briefly before him; then touches his shoulder and crosses to downstage center.*]

ZELDA [*her back to the feared bush*]: The incredible things are the only true things, Scott. Why do you have to go mad to make a discovery as simple as that? Who is fooling whom with this pretense that to exist is a credible thing? The mad are not so gullible. We're not taken in by such a transparent falsity, oh, no, what we know that you don't know— [*She is now facing the audience.*] Or don't dare admit that you know is that to exist is the original and greatest of incredible things. Between the first wail of an infant and the last gasp of the dying—it's all an arranged pattern of—submission to what's been prescribed for us unless we escape into madness or into acts of creation. . . . The latter option was denied me, Scott, by someone not a thousand miles from here. [*She faces Scott.*] Look at what was left me!

scott: I thought you'd gone in to dinner.

zelda: I won't be forced to dine at five o'clock, especially with a visitor still on the grounds. I have not forgotten all manners, after all . . .

[*She goes to the bench.*]

scott: Then sit down a while.

zelda: Help me turn the bench away from that flaming bush.

[*He rises and they turn the bench at a sharper angle. She then sits beside him, holding his hand, caressing his faded hair.*]

—As I grew older, Goofo, the losses accumulated in my heart, the disenchantments steadily increased. That's usual, yes? Simply the process of aging. —Adjustments had to be made to faiths that had faded as candles into daybreak. In their place, what? Sharp light cast on things that appalled me, that blew my mind out, Goofo. Then. —The wisdom, the sorrowful wisdom of acceptance. Wouldn't accept it. Romantics won't, you know. Liquor, madness, more or less the same thing. We're abandoned or we're put away, and if put away, why, then, fantasy runs riot, hallucinations bring back times lost. Loves you'd frightened away return in dreams. —A remission occurs. You fall out of a cloud to what's called real—a rock! Cold, barren. To be endured only briefly. —Goofo? The last time I was home with Mother in Montgomery I used to ride the trolley car to the end of the line and back again, going nowhere, just going. Someone asked me one time, "Why do you do that?" and I said, "Just for something to do." —Yes, I went back to the world of vision which was my only true home. I said to Mother, the last time I told her good-bye, "Don't worry about me. I'm not afraid to die." —Why were *you* afraid to? The sentence is imposed—there's no appeal, no reprieve!—Don't be so gutless about it.

SCOTT: Zelda, haven't you something more comforting to offer me on this cold, windy hilltop than—worn-out recriminations?

[*She rises and picks up her coat.*]

ZELDA: I offer you my horse blanket, Scott. And in return for its comfort, I have to make a request, a last one, of you. —If there should be nine mounds of indistinguishable ash at the barred door up there, persuade them somehow to scatter all to the wind to be blown out to sea: that's the purification, *give me that!* God damn you, enemy, love, *give—me—that!*

[*He frees himself from her fierce hands and rises, breathing heavily.*]

Oh, dear you're agitated. Is it the prospect of writing a film for the Crawford? She's not Eleanora Duse nor even Bernhardt but she has her own territory that she'll fight hard to hold and she'll hold it a while. —I only mentioned her, Goofo, to show a bit of polite interest in things at the Garden of Allah, and look, you're all worked up—not good for a failing heart. Didn't you say you'd had frightening attacks of—?

SCOTT: You must have—misunderstood me.

ZELDA: Oh. Good. I'm relieved.

SCOTT: This *is* a windy hilltop.

ZELDA: Serious conversation's wasted, it's blown away. So let's return to the cheerful little idiocies that we began with.

SCOTT: They were blown away, too.

ZELDA: You're shivering, you're still breathing too rapidly over the Crawford assignment.

[*She attempts to draw the shapeless coat about him; he hurls it away again. The action dizzies him; he clutches hold of the bench.*]

Why, Scott! You're as dizzy as I was when I attempted the *pizzicato*! Let's—stretch out on the grass like we used to after picnics—*au bord de l'Oise* . . .

[*He shakes his head helplessly.*]

Breathe quietly, rest. [*She takes hold of his wrist.*] —Where's your pulse? I can't feel your pulse.

SCOTT: Never mind . . .

ZELDA: Somebody has to point out to you these little physical symptoms, not to alarm you but—

SCOTT [*exploding involuntarily*]: You've pointed out to me nothing I haven't observed myself. —The mistake of our ever having met! —The monumental error of the effort to channel our lives together in an institution called marriage. Tragic for us both. Result—slag heap of a—dream . . .

ZELDA: Poor Scott.

SCOTT: Meaning "poor son of a bitch."

ZELDA: What a way to speak of your irreproachably proper mother!

SCOTT: CUT!

ZELDA: What?

SCOTT: That's what a film director shouts when a scene is finished . . .

ZELDA: Finished, is it? The visitor's bell has rung and we can withdraw to our separate worlds now?

[*She throws back her head and shouts "CUT!" He attempts to rise from the bench, gasps, and falls back onto it. The intern advances rapidly to Zelda and takes hold of her hand.*]

INTERN: What is it, Zelda? Why'd you shout like that?

ZELDA: This gentleman on the bench was once my husband and I was once his wife, sort of a storybook marriage, legendary. Yes, well, legends fade. It seems he's finally faced that. He just now admitted that despite its ideal, relentlessly public appearance, it had been, I quote him, a monumental error, and that it had been a mistake for us ever to have met. Something's been accomplished: a recognition—painful, but good therapy's often painful.

SCOTT: Let go of her hand. She isn't yours.

ZELDA: Oh, yes, I was his once. You didn't hear the confession, or did you doubt the truth of it?

SCOTT [*trembling*]: I said let go of her hand. Remember you're just employed here.

INTERN: Employed to care for patients.

ZELDA: Scott used to be quicker at games.

SCOTT: LET GO OF HER HAND, I SAID! God damn it, let her hand go, or I'll have you discharged.

ZELDA: —Neither of us is cruel but we're hurting each other unbearably. Can't you stop it?

INTERN: Visiting hours are nearly over. [*He rises and starts away.*]

SCOTT: Hold on a moment more! Maybe *you* can explain to her the advantage she's had in being psychotic, since it seems you've acquired, by means I won't inquire into—

ZELDA: Advise him to remain—

INTERN: Let him speak it out.

ZELDA: Within the safe, sunny woodlands called Holly, not to venture into—

SCOTT: Oh, I've known darker places, I've been places where it's always—

ZELDA: Three o'clock in the morning? Dark night of the soul again?

[*Overlap.*]

SCOTT: Followed you but went further—without escort or guide or protector . . .

ZELDA: Oh, not caught and led into and locked! For incineration?

INTERN: Zelda!

75

[*Scott clenches his fists impotently.*]

SCOTT: The name of this woman—

ZELDA: Once known as a lady.

SCOTT: Is still Mrs. F. Scott Fitzgerald.

ZELDA: As distinguished from Lily Sheil? —As acceptable insult, leaves me quite unabashed.

INTERN: Mr. Fitzgerald, it's permissible to leave before visiting hours are over, and the—

ZELDA: Iron gates are closed . . .

INTERN: Zelda? [*He extends his hand to her.*]

ZELDA: How sweet of Scott to have flown such a long way to see me. A delightful surprise to find myself still remembered by an old beau that I thought must have filed me away long ago among his—fantasies discarded . . .

SISTERS [*at the gate*]: Visiting hours are over. The gates are about to be closed.

SCOTT: Allow me a moment or two with my wife alone.

INTERN: A moment only. Your visit has disturbed her, Mr. Fitzgerald. [*He enters the asylum.*]

ZELDA [*following intern*]: Such a fiery sunset . . .

[*Scott stumbles toward her.*]

What are you following me for?

SCOTT: Taking you to the gates.

ZELDA: The gates are iron, they won't admit you or ever release me again. [*She enters; the gates close.*] I'm not your book! Anymore! *I can't be your book anymore! Write yourself a new book!*

SCOTT [*reaching desperately through the bars*]: The ring, please take it, the covenant with the past— [*She disappears.*] —still always present, Zelda!

[*A wind seems to sweep him back as the stage dims slowly. Mist drifts in. Scott turns downstage; his haunted eyes ask a silent question which he must know cannot be answered.*]

THE END

Some New Directions Paperbooks

For complete listing request complete catalog from
New Directions, 80 Eighth Avenue, New York 10011   † Bilingual